For Joe
~ IO

For Grandad and
Grandpa, with love x
~ KR

CATERPILLAR BOOKS

An imprint of the Little Tiger Group

www.littletiger.co.uk

1 Coda Studios, 189 Munster Road, London SW6 6AW

First published in Great Britain 2018

Text by Isabel Otter • Text copyright © Caterpillar Books 2018

Illustrations copyright © Katie Rewse 2018

All rights reserved • Printed in China

ISBN: 978-1-84857-713-8

CPB/1800/0867/0418

2 4 6 8 10 9 7 5 3 1

# The GARDEN of HOPE

Isabel Otter    Katie Rewse

Things had changed since Mum had been gone.
The house was untidy.
Maya, Dad and Pip were a bit of a mess.


And the garden had become wild and overgrown.

Dad was trying his best, but sometimes it was hard to remember all the things that needed doing!

Maya sometimes felt lonely, but luckily she had Pip. Of course, there were moments when it was impossible not to miss Mum.

When Maya felt sad, Dad was always there for a bear hug.
He was a great storyteller, and he told Maya tales of magic and adventures in faraway lands. She particularly enjoyed the stories when Dad wove her and Pip into the plot as brave characters.

One afternoon, Maya was feeling sad, and a little bit anxious.

Dad said it was time for a story. This one was going to be about Mum. Maya stopped biting her nails and looked up; Dad hardly ever told stories about Mum.

"You know your mum used to worry about things too, don't you Maya?" said Dad. "Whenever she felt upset, she would go outside, plant some seeds and wait for them to grow into something new and beautiful. Your mum knew that by the time the seeds had grown, those worries would have faded away. She called them her seeds of hope."

On the table were several packets of seeds. Dad and Maya looked out at the overgrown garden and shared a smile.

Maya started in the potting shed.
It was full of dust and cobwebs but she soon found what she needed.

Next, she began to busily pull up weeds. The garden had been unloved for a long time and the weeds had tangled themselves over everything!

At last, the ground was ready. It was time to plant
the first seed. Maya chose the packet with a bright
sunflower on the front. It was Mum's favourite flower.

As she dug a hole, Maya thought about Dad's story.
She dropped the first seed in,
closed her eyes
and hoped.

Some days were harder than others for Maya, but thinking about the garden made her feel calm. When the first small green shoot appeared, Maya felt a rush of happiness.

The seed had become
something new and beautiful.

Sometimes, Pip tried to help in his own way...

Luckily, holes could
always be filled in again.

Sometimes Dad felt angry or upset,
and then he joined Maya in the garden
and they planted seeds together.

Buds were starting to appear on some of the plants.
Maya spent all her spare time outside, rain or shine,
nurturing her garden.

In turn, the garden repaid
Maya's love by making her feel
lighter and happier than she
had felt in a very long time.

Maya now had some fully grown plants and flowers as well as seedlings.
The flowers began to bloom and this attracted new visitors.

First came the bees and the butterflies...

Then came ladybirds, dragonflies and beetles...

Birds arrived, and with them voles and hedgehogs...

Finally came rabbits, squirrels and foxes.

The garden was humming, hopping, buzzing and bursting with life!

Maya had transformed the garden
into a place of beauty once more.

Mum had been right; Maya had forgotten
the worries she had planted with the
seeds. The garden had carried them away.

Things had changed since Mum had been gone.
The house was still untidy.
Maya, Dad and Pip were still rather a mess.

But something felt different...
For the first time in a long while, there was hope.

Dad and Maya looked out at their
beautiful garden and shared a smile.